♥

This book belongs to:

....
....

♥

Dear Parents,

'When Grandpa Died' is aimed at humanist parents who wish to introduce the topics of death, bereavement and organ donation to very young children in a factual manner. This book uses simple truthful words to explain what happens when someone dies. It offers reassurance to a bereaved child by encouraging the child to remember the bereaved person via memories by drawing pictures and by reinstating that the child and their family essentially remain safe.

♥

When Grandpa Died

Mummy was crying.

She told me that Grandpa had died.

♥

I tried to poke Grandpa, but he did

not stir.

I started to cry.

♥

Mummy told me that Grandpa will

never wake up.

He will not walk or

eat or

poop or

do anything else.

♥

He will not be coming back.

Not even for my birthday!

♥

I wanted Grandpa to wake up.

I wanted to hear him laugh.

I wanted him to tickle my tummy.

I wanted to hear his stories.

But that is not going to happen now.

♥

Mummy told me that when people

die their bodies slowly become

dust.

Plants and animals die too.

I cried loudly.

Mummy told me that it was all right to cry.

She cried too.

We comforted each other.

Grandpa died because his body

stopped working.

That happens sometimes.

He cannot feel pain now and that is

good.

Sometimes sad things happen.

But it is all right.

Mummy said that I was safe.

She was safe.

There was no need to worry.

♥

Grandpa does not need his eyes now.

He had decided to give them away long ago.

He had told Mummy about this.

Some doctors came around to perform a quick operation and took his eyes away.

Grandpa did not feel any pain.

♥

He looked just the same.

His eyes will be given to a sightless person.

It will be Grandpa's gift.

Grandpa was always kind.

Grandpa was taken away.

I said good-bye to him.

I miss him.

Mummy misses him too!

We now remember Grandpa by talking about him.

We think of all the fun things that we did together.

Sometimes we cry.

Sometimes we laugh.

And that feels nice.

♥

I think of Grandpa often.

Whenever I miss him

I draw a picture of him.

That makes Mummy smile.

It makes me smile too.

♥

I will always love him.

A lot!

Printed in Great Britain
by Amazon

41003216R00018